DATE DUE

OCT 1 1997	1 2 APR 1999
OCT 3 1997	MAR 1 4
OCT 2 1997	
NOV 1 1997	
FEB 1 4 1998	
SEP 1 1 1998	
0 8 DEC 1998	
2 2 FEB 1999	
2 MAR 1999	

CREATIVE'S CLASSIC STORIES

This short story is taken out of an anthology and presented in its own volume where it stands a better chance of being read and remembered.

In one story, we might see a character survive extreme loneliness, danger, or sadness. Reading about such characters and events can be a powerful experience. And once we've read a good story, it can stay dormant in our memories for years and come to the surface later when we need its wisdom in facing our own danger, loneliness or sadness.

This short story is a well-told classic which has stood the test of time. It is included in Creative's Classic Stories Series and presented with all the dignity and richness a good classic story deserves.

THE MAN THAT
CORRUPTED HADLEYBURG

THE MAN THAT CORRUPTED HADLEYBURG

MARK TWAIN

Creative Education, Inc.
Mankato, Minnesota

Published by Creative Education, Inc.
123 South Broad Street, Mankato, Minnesota 56001

Copyright ©1986 by Creative Education, Inc. International copyrights
reserved in all countries. No part of this book may be reproduced in any
form without written permission from the publisher.
Printed in the United States.

Library of Congress Cataloging-in-Publication Data

Twain, Mark, 1835-1910.
  The Man That Corrupted Hadleyburg.

  (Creative's classic short stories)
  Summary: A stranger who feels mistreated by a supposedly incorruptible town
concocts a vengeful scheme to test the honesty of its leading citizens.
  [1. Honesty—Fiction.   2. City and town life—Fiction]   I. Title.   II. Series.
PZ7.C584Man   1986   [Fic]   86-6164
ISBN 0-88682-006-5

To

the continuation of fine literature

for readers of all ages.

It was many years ago. Hadleyburg was the most honest and upright town in all the region round about. It had kept that reputation unsmirched during three generations, and was prouder of it than of any other of its possessions. It was so proud of it, and so anxious to insure its perpetuation, that it began to teach the principles of honest dealing to its babies in the cradle, and made the like teachings the staple of their culture thenceforward through all the years devoted to their education. Also, throughout the formative years temptations were kept out of the way of the young people, so that their honesty could have every chance to harden and solidify, and become a part of their very bone. The neighboring towns were jealous of this honorable supremacy, and affected to sneer at Hadleyburg's pride in it and call it vanity; but all the same they were obliged to acknowledge that Hadleyburg was in reality an incorruptible town; and if pressed they would also acknowledge that the mere fact that a young man hailed from Hadleyburg was all the recommendation he needed when he went forth from his natal town to seek for responsible employment.

But at last, in the drift of time, Hadleyburg had the ill luck to offend a passing stranger — possibly without knowing it, certainly without caring, for Hadleyburg was sufficient unto itself, and cared not a rap for strangers or their opinions. Still, it would have been well to make an exception in this one's case, for he was a bitter man and revengeful. All through his wanderings during a whole year he kept his injury in mind, and gave all his leisure moments to try-

ing to invent a compensating satisfaction for it. He con-
trived many plans, and all of them were good, but none
of them was quite sweeping enough; the poorest of them
would hurt a great many individuals, but what he wanted
was a plan which would comprehend the entire town, and
not let so much as one person escape unhurt. At last he
had a fortunate idea, and when it fell into his brain it lit
up his whole head with an evil joy. He began to form a
plan at once, saying to himself, "That is the thing to do—
I will corrupt the town."

Six months later he went to Hadleyburg, and arrived
in a buggy at the house of the old cashier of the bank about
ten at night. He got a sack out of the buggy, shouldered
it, and staggered with it through the cottage yard, and
knocked at the door. A woman's voice said "Come in,"
and he entered, and set his sack behind the stove in the
parlor, saying politely to the old lady who sat reading the

Missionary Herald by the lamp:

"Pray keep your seat, madam, I will not disturb you. There — now it is pretty well concealed; one would hardly know it was there. Can I see your husband a moment, madam?"

No, he was gone to Brixton, and might not return before morning.

"Very well, madam, it is no matter. I merely wanted to leave that sack in his care, to be delivered to the rightful owner when he shall be found. I am a stranger; he does not know me; I am merely passing through the town tonight to discharge a matter which has been long in my mind. My errand is now completed, and I go pleased and a little proud, and you will never see me again. There is a paper attached to the sack which will explain everything. Good-night, madam."

The old lady was afraid of the mysterious big stranger,

and was glad to see him go. But her curiosity was roused, and she went straight to the sack and brought away the paper. It began as follows:

"*TO BE PUBLISHED; or, the right man sought out by private inquiry — either will answer. This sack contains gold coin weighing a hundred and sixty pounds four ounces —* "

"Mercy on us, and the door not locked!"

Mrs. Richards flew to it all in a tremble and locked it, then pulled down the window shades and stood frightened, worried, and wondering if there was anything else she could do toward making herself and the money more safe. She listened awhile for burglars, then surrendered to curiosity and went back to the lamp and finished reading the paper:

"*I am a foreigner, and am presently going back to my own country, to remain there permanently. I am grateful to America for what I have received at her hands during my stay under her flag; and to one of her citizens — a citizen of Hadleyburg — I am especially grateful for a great kindness done me a year or two ago. Two great kindnesses; in fact. I will explain. I was a gambler. I say I WAS. I was a ruined gambler. I arrived in this village at night, hungry and without a penny. I asked for help — in the dark; I was ashamed to beg in the light. I begged of the right man. He gave me twenty dollars — that is to say, he gave me life, as I considered it. He also gave me fortune; for out of that money I have made myself rich at the gaming-table. And finally, a remark which he made to me has remained with me to this day, and has at last conquered me; and in conquering has saved the remnant of my morals; I shall gamble no more. Now I have no idea who that man was, but I want him found, and I want him to have this money, to give away, throw away or keep, as he pleases. It is merely my way of testifying my gratitude to him. If I could stay, I would find him myself;*

but no matter, he will be found. This is an honest town, an incorruptible town, and I know I can trust it without fear. This man can be identified by the remark which he made to me; I feel persuaded that he will remember it.

"And now my plan is this: If you prefer to conduct the in-quiry privately, do so. Tell the contents of this present writing to any one who is likely to be the right man. If he shall answer, 'I am the man; the remark I made was so-and-so,' apply the test—to wit: open the sack, and in it you will find a sealed envelope containing that remark. If the remark mentioned by the candidate tallies with it, give him the money, and ask no further questions, for he is certainly the right man.

"But if you shall prefer a public inquiry, then publish this present writing in the local paper — with these instructions added, to wit: Thirty days from now, let the candidate appear at the town hall at eight in the evening (Friday), and

hand his remark, in a sealed envelope, to the Rev. Mr. Burgess (if he will be kind enough to act); and let Mr. Burgess
there and then destroy the seals on the sack, open it, and see
if the remark is correct; if correct, let the money be delivered, with my sincere gratitude, to my benefactor thus
identified."

Mrs. Richards sat down, gently, quivering with excitement and was soon lost in thinking — after this pattern:
"What a strange thing it is! — And what a fortune for that
kind man who set his bread afloat upon the waters!. . .If
he had only been my husband that did it! — for we are so
poor, so old and poor!. . ." Then, with a sigh — "But it was
not my Edward; no, it was not he that gave the stranger
twenty dollars. It is a pity too; I see it now. . ." Then, with
a shudder — "But it is *gambler's* money! the wages of sin:
we couldn't take it; we couldn't touch it. I don't like to
be near it; it seems a defilement." She moved to a farther

chair... "I wish Edward would come, and take it to the bank; a burglar might come at any moment; it is dreadful to be here all alone with it."

At eleven Mr. Richards arrived, and while his wife was saying, "I am *so* glad you've come!" he was saying, "I'm so tired — tired clear out; it is dreadful to be poor, and have to make these dismal journeys at my time of life. Always at the grind, grind, grind, on a salary — another man's slave, and he sitting at home in his slippers, right and comfortable."

I am so sorry for you, Edward, you know that; but be comforted; we have our livelihood; we have our good name—"

"Yes, Mary, and that is everything. Don't mind my talk — it's just a moment's irritation and doesn't mean anything. Kiss me — there, it's all gone now, and I am not complaining any more. What have you been getting?

What's in the sack?"

Then his wife told him the great secret. It dazed him for a moment; then he said:

"It weighs a hundred and sixty pounds? Why, Mary, it's for-ty thou-sand dollars — think of it — a whole fortune! Not ten men in this village are worth that much. Give me the paper."

He skimmed through it and said:

"Isn't it an adventure! Why, it's a romance; it's like the impossible things one reads about in books, and never sees in life." He was well stirred up now; cheerful, even gleeful. He tapped his old wife on the cheek, and said, humorously, "Why, we're rich, Mary, rich; all we've got to do is to bury the money and burn the papers. If the gambler ever comes to inquire, we'll merely look coldly upon him and say: 'What is this nonsense you are talking: We have never heard of you and your sack of gold before;' and then he would look foolish, and —"

"And in the mean time, while you are running on with your jokes, the money is still here, and it is fast getting along toward burglar-time."

"True, Very well, what shall we do — make the inquiry private? No, not that: it would spoil the romance. The public method is better. Think what a noise it will make! And it will make all the other towns jealous; for no stranger would trust such a thing to any town but Hadleyburg, and they know it. It's a great card for us. I must get to the printing office now, or I shall be too late."

"But stop — stop — don't leave me here alone with it, Edward!"

But he was gone. For only a little while, however. Not far from his own house he met the editor-proprietor of the paper, and gave him the document, and said, "Here is a good thing for you, Cox — put it in."

"It may be too late, Mr. Richards, but I'll see."

At home again he and his wife sat down to talk the charming mystery over; they were in no condition for sleep. The first question was, Who could the citizen have been who gave the stranger the twenty dollars? It seemed a simple one; both answered it in the same breath —

"Barclay Goodson."

"Yes," said Richards, "he could have done it, and it would have been like him, but there's not another in the town."

"Everybody will grant that, Edward — grant it privately, anyway. For six months, now, the village has been its own proper self once more — honest, narrow, self-righteous, and stingy."

"It is what he always called it, to the day of his death — said it right out publicly, too."

"Yes, and he was hated for it."

"Oh, of course; but he didn't care. I reckon he was the best-hated man among us, except the Reverend Burgess."

"Well, Burgess deserves it — he will never get another congregation here. Mean as the town is, it knows how to estimate *him*. Edward, doesn't it seem odd that the stranger should appoint Burgess to deliver the money?"

"Well, yes — it does. That is — that is —"

"Why so much that-*is*-ing? Would *you* select him?"

"Mary, maybe the stranger knows him better than this village does."

"Much *that* would help Burgess!"

The husband seemed perplexed for an answer; the wife kept a steady eye upon him, and waited. Finally Richards said, with the hesitancy of one who is making a statement which is likely to encounter doubt:

"Mary, Burgess is not a bad man."

His wife was certainly surprised.

"Nonsense!" she exclaimed.

"He is not a bad man. I know. The whole of his un-popularity had its foundation in that one thing — the thing that made so much noise."

"That 'one thing,' indeed! As if that 'one thing' wasn't enough, all by itself."

"Plenty. Plenty. Only he wasn't guilty of it."

"How you talk! Not guilty of it! Everybody knows he *was* guilty."

"Mary, I give you my word — he was innocent."

"I can't believe it, and I don't. How do you know?"

"It is a confession. I am ashamed, but I will make it. I was the only man who knew he was innocent. I could have saved him, and — and — well, you know how the town was wrought up — I hadn't the pluck to do it. It would have turned everybody against me. I felt mean, ever so mean; but I didn't dare; I hadn't the manliness to face that."

Mary looked troubled, and for a while was silent. Then she said, stammeringly:

"I — I don't think it would have done for you to — to— One mustn't — er — public opinion — one has to be so careful — so —" It was a difficult road, and she got mired; but after a little she got started again. "It was a great pity, but — Why, we couldn't afford it, Edward — we couldn't indeed. Oh, I wouldn't have had you do it for anything!"

"It would have lost us the good will of so many people, Mary; and then — and then —"

"What troubles me now is, what *he* thinks of us, Edward."

"He? *He* doesn't suspect that I could have saved him."

"Oh," exclaimed the wife, in a tone of relief, "I am glad of that. As long as he doesn't know that you could have saved him, he — he — well, that makes it a great deal better. Why, I might have known he didn't know, because

he is always trying to be friendly with us, as little encourage-
ment as we give him. More than once people have twitted
me with it. There's the Wilsons, and the Wilcoxes, and the
Harknesses, they take a mean pleasure in saying, 'Your
friend Burgess,' because they know it pesters me. I wish he
wouldn't persist in liking us so; I can't think why he keeps
it up."

"I can explain it. It's another confession. When the
thing was new and hot, and the town made a plan to ride
him on a rail, my conscience hurt me so that I couldn't stand
it, and I went privately and gave him notice, and he got
out of the town and stayed out till it was safe to come back."

"Edward! If the town had found it out —"

"*Don't!* It scares me yet, to think of it. I repented of
it the minute it was done; and I was even afraid to tell you,
lest your face might betray it to somebody. I didn't sleep
any that night, for worrying. But after a few days I saw that

no one was going to suspect me, and after that I got to feeling glad I did it. And I feel glad yet, Mary — glad through and through."

"So do I, now, for it would have been a dreadful way to treat him. Yes, I'm glad; for really you did owe him that, you know. But, Edward, suppose it should come out yet, some day!"

"It won't."

"Why!"

"Because everybody thinks it was Goodson."

"Of course they would!"

"Certainly. And of course *he* didn't care. They persuaded poor old Sawlsberry to go and charge it on him, and he went blustering over there and did it. Goodson looked him over, like as if he was hunting for a place on him that he could despise the most, then he says, 'So you are the Committee of Inquiry, are you?' Sawlsberry said that was about what he was. 'Hm. Do they require particulars, or do you reckon a kind of a *general* answer will do?' 'If they require particulars, I will come back, Mr. Goodson; I will take the general answer first.' 'Very well, then, tell them to go to hell — I reckon that's general enough. And I'll give you some advice, Sawlsberry; when you come back for the particulars, fetch a basket to carry the relics of yourself home in.' "

"Just like Goodson; it's got all the marks. He had only vanity; he thought he could give advice better than any other person."

"It settled the business, and saved us, Mary. The subject was dropped."

"Bless you, I'm not doubting *that*."

Then they took up the gold-sack mystery again, with strong interest. Soon the conversation began to suffer breaks — interruptions caused by absorbed thinkings. The breaks grew more and more frequent. At last Richards lost himself wholly in thought. He sat long, gazing vacantly at the floor, and by-and-by he began to punctuate his thoughts with little nervous movements of his hands that seemed to indicate vexation. Meantime his wife too had relapsed into a thoughtful silence, and her movements were beginning to show a troubled discomfort. Finally Richards got up and strode aimlessly about the room, ploughing his hands through his hair, much as a somnambulist might do who was having a bad dream. Then he seemed to arrive at a definite purpose; and without a word he put on his hat and passed quickly out of the house. His wife sat brooding, with a drawn face, and did not seem to be aware that she was alone. Now and then she murmured, "Lead us not in t . . . but — but — we are so poor, so poor! . . . Lead us not into . . . Ah, who would be hurt by it? — and no one would ever know . . . Lead us . . ." The voice died out in mumblings.

After a little she glanced up and muttered in a half frightened, half-glad way —

"He is gone! But, oh dear, he may be too late — too
late...Maybe not — maybe there is still time." She rose
and stood thinking, nervously clasping and unclasping her
hands. A slight shudder shook her frame, and she said, out
of a dry throat, "God forgive me — it's awful to think such
things — but...Lord, how we are made — how strangely
we are made!"

She turned the light low, and slipped stealthily over and
kneeled down by the sack and felt of its ridgy sides with
her hands, and fondled them lovingly; and there was a
gloating light in her poor old eyes. She fell into fits of
absence; and came half out of them at times to mutter, "If
we had only waited! — oh, if we had only waited a little,
and not been in such a hurry!"

Meantime Cox had gone home from his office and told

his wife all about the strange thing that had happened, and they had talked it over eagerly, and guessed that the late Goodson was the only man in the town who could have helped a suffering stranger with so noble a sum as twenty dollars. Then there was a pause, and the two became thoughtful and silent. And by-and-by nervous and fidgety. At last the wife said, as if to herself:

"Nobody knows this secret but the Richardses...and us...nobody."

The husband came out of his thinkings with a slight start, and gazed wistfully at his wife, whose face was become very pale; then he hesitatingly rose, and glanced furtively at his hat, then at his wife — a sort of mute inquiry. Mrs. Cox swallowed once or twice, with her hand at her throat, then in place of speech she nodded her head. In a moment she was alone, and mumbling to herself.

And now Richards and Cox were hurrying through the

deserted streets, from opposite directions. They met, panting, at the foot of the printing-office stairs; by the night-light there they read each other's face. Cox whispered:

"Nobody knows about this but us?"

The whispered answer was,

"Not a soul — on honor, not a soul!"

"If it isn't too late to —"

The men were starting upstairs; at this moment they were overtaken by a boy, and Cox asked:

"Is that you, Johnny?"

"Yes, sir."

"You needn't ship the early mail — nor *any* mail; wait till I tell you."

"It's already gone, sir."

"*Gone?*" It had the sound of an unspeakable disappointment in it.

"Yes, sir. Time-table for Brixton and all the towns

beyond changed today, sir — had to get the papers in twenty minutes earlier than common. I had to rush; if I had been two minutes later —"

The men turned and walked slowly away, not waiting to hear the rest. Neither of them spoke during ten minutes; then Cox said, in a vexed tone:

"What possessed you to be in such a hurry, *I* can't make out."

"The answer was humble enough:

"I see it now, but somehow I never thought, you know, until it was too late. But the next time —"

"Next time be hanged! It won't come in a thousand years."

Then the friends separated without a good-night, and dragged themselves home with the gait of mortally stricken men. At their homes their wives sprang up with an eager "Well?" — then saw the answer with their eyes and sank down sorrowing, without waiting for it to come in words. In both houses a discussion followed of a heated sort — a new thing; there had been discussions before, but not heated ones, not ungentle ones. The discussions tonight were a sort of seeming plagiarisms of each other. Mrs. Richards said,

"If you had only waited, Edward — if you had only stopped to think; but no, you must run straight to the printing office and spread it all over the world."

"It *said* publish it."

"That is nothing; it also said do it privately, if you liked. There, now — is that true, or not?"

"Why, yes — yes, it is true, but when I thought what a stir it would make, and what a compliment it was to Hadleyburg that a stranger should trust it so —"

"Oh, certainly, I know all that; but if you had only stopped to think, you would have seen that you *couldn't* find the right man, because he is in his grave, and hasn't left chick nor child nor relation behind him; and as long as the money went to somebody that awfully needed it, and nobody would be hurt by it, and — and —"

She broke down, crying. Her husband tried to think of some comforting thing to say, and presently came out with this:

"But after all, Mary, it must be for the best — it *must* be; we know that. And we must remember that it was so ordered —"

"Ordered! Oh, everything's *ordered*, when a person has to find some way out when he has been stupid. Just the same, it was *ordered* that the money should come to us in this special way, and it was you that must take it on yourself to go meddling with the designs of Providence — and who gave you the right? It was wicked, that is what it was — just blasphemous presumption, and no more becoming to a meek and humble professor of —"

"But, Mary, you know how we have been trained all our lives long, like the whole village, till it is absolutely second nature to us to stop not a single moment to think when there's an honest thing to be done —"

"Oh, I know it, I know it — it's been one everlasting training and training and training in honesty — honesty shielded, from the very cradle, against every possible temptation, and so it's *artificial* honesty, and weak as water when temptation comes, as we have seen this night. God knows I never had shade nor shadow of a doubt of my petrified and indestructible honesty until now — and now, under the very first big and real temptation, I — Edward, it is my belief that this town's honesty is as rotten as mine is; as rotten as yours is. It is a mean town, a hard, stingy town, and hasn't a virtue in the world but this honesty it is so celebrated for and so conceited about; and so help me, I do believe that if ever the day comes that its honesty falls under great temptation, its grand reputation will go to ruin like a house of cards. There, now, I've made confession, and I feel better; I am a humbug, and I've been one all my life, without knowing it. Let no man call me honest again — I will not have it."

"I — Well, Mary, I feel a good deal as you do; I certainly do. It seems strange, too, so strange. I never could have believed it — never."

A long silence followed; both were sunk in thought. At last the wife looked up and said:

"I know what you are thinking, Edward."

Richards had the embarrassed look of a person who is caught.

"I am ashamed to confess it, Mary, but —"

"It's no matter, Edward, I was thinking the same question myself."

"I hope so. State it."

"You were thinking, if a body could only guess out *what the remark was* that Goodson made to the stranger."

"It's perfectly true. I feel guilty and ashamed. And you?"

"I'm past it. Let us make a pallet here; we've got to stand watch till the bank vault opens in the morning and admits the sack...Oh, dear, oh, dear — if we hadn't made the mistake!"

The pallet was made, and Mary said:

"The open sesame — what could it have been? I do wonder what that remark could have been? But come; we will get to bed now."

"And sleep?"

"No, think."

"Yes, think."

By this time the Coxes too had completed their spat

and their reconciliation, and were turning in — to think, to think, and toss, and fret, and worry over what the remark could possibly have been which Goodson made to the stranded derelict: that golden remark; that remark worth forty thousand dollars, cash.

The reason that the village telegraph office was open later than usual that night was this: The foreman of Cox's paper was the local representative of the Associated Press. One might say its honorary representative, for it wasn't four times a year that he could furnish thirty words that would be accepted. But this time it was different. His despatch stating what he had caught got an instant answer:

"Send the whole thing — all the details — twelve hundred words."

A colossal order! The foreman filled the bill; and he was the proudest man in the State. By breakfast-time the next morning the name of Hadleyburg the Incorruptible was on every lip in America, from Montreal to the Gulf, from the glaciers of Alaska to the orange groves of Florida; and millions and millions of people were discussing the stranger and his money-sack, and wondering if the right man would be found, and hoping some more news about the matter would come soon — right away.

Chapter 2

Hadleyburg village woke up world-celebrated — astonished — happy — vain. Vain beyond imagination. Its nineteen principal citizens and their wives went about shaking hands with each other, and beaming, and smiling, and congratulating, and saying *this* thing adds a new word to the dictionary — *Hadleyburg*, synonym for *incorruptible* — destined to live in dictionaries forever! And the minor and unimportant citizens and their wives went around acting in much the same way. Everybody ran to the bank to see the gold-sack; and before noon grieved and envious crowds began to flock in from Brixton and all the neighboring towns; and that afternoon and next day reporters began to arrive from everywhere to verify the sack and its history and write the whole thing up anew, and make dashing free-hand pictures of the sack and of Richards' house, and the bank, and the Presbyterian church, and the Baptist church, and the public square, and the town hall where the test would be applied and the money delivered; and damnable portraits of the Richardses, and Pinkerton the banker, and Cox, and the foreman, and Reverend Burgess, and the postmaster — and even of Jack Halliday, who was the loafing, goodnatured, no-account, irreverent fisherman, hunter, boys' friend, stray-dog's friend, typical "Sam Lawson" of the town. The little mean, smirking, oily Pinkerton showed the sack to all comers, and rubbed his sleek palms together pleasantly, and enlarged upon the town's fine old reputation for honesty and upon this wonderful endorsement of it, and hoped and believed that the example would now spread far and wide over the American world, and be epoch-making in the matter of moral regeneration. And so on, and so on.

By the end of a week things had quieted down again; the wild intoxication of pride and joy had sobered to a soft, sweet, silent delight — a sort of deep, nameless, unutterable content. All faces bore a look of peaceful, holy happiness.

Then a change came. It was a gradual change: so gradual that its beginnings were hardly noticed; maybe were not noticed at all, except by Jack Halliday, who always noticed everything; and always made fun of it, too, no matter what it was. He began to throw out chaffing remarks about people not looking quite so happy as they did a day or two ago; and next he claimed that the new aspect was deepening to positive sadness; next, that it was taking on a sick look; and finally he said that everybody was become so moody, thoughtful, and absent-minded that he could rob the meanest man in town of a cent out of the bottom of his breeches pocket and not disturb his revery.

At this stage — or at about this stage — a saying like

this was dropped at bedtime — with a sigh, usually — by the head of each of the nineteen principal households: "Ah, what *could* have been the remark that Goodson made!"

And straightway — with a shudder — came this, from the man's wife:

"Oh, *don't!* What horrible thing are you mulling in your mind? Put it away from you, for God's sake!"

But that question was wrung from those men again the next night — and got the same retort. But weaker.

And the third night the men uttered the question yet again — with anguish, and absently. This time — and the following night — the wives fidgeted feebly, and tried to say something. But didn't.

And the night after that they found their tongues and responded — longingly,

"Oh, if we *could* only guess!"

Halliday's comments grew daily more and more spar-

klingly disagreeable and disparaging. He went diligently
about, laughing at the town, individually and in mass. But
his laugh was the only one left in the village: it fell upon
a hollow and mournful vacancy and emptiness. Not even
a smile was findable anywhere. Halliday carried a cigar box
around on a tripod, playing that it was a camera, and halted
all passers and aimed the thing and said, "Ready! — now
look pleasant, please," but not even this capital joke could
surprise the dreary faces into any softening.

So three weeks passed — one week was left. It was Saturday evening — after supper. Instead of the aforetime Saturday evening flutter and bustle and shopping and larking,
the streets were empty and desolate. Richards and his old
wife sat apart in their little parlor — miserable and thinking. This was becoming their evening habit now: the life-
long habit which preceded it, of reading, knitting, and contented chat, or receiving or paying neighborly calls, was

dead and gone and forgotten, ages ago — two or three weeks ago; nobody talked now, nobody read, nobody visited — the whole village sat at home, sighing, worrying, silent. Trying to guess out that remark.

The postman left a letter. Richards glanced listlessly at the superscription and the post-mark — unfamiliar, both — and tossed the letter on the table and resumed his might-have-beens and his hopeless dull miseries where he had left them off. Two or three hours later his wife got wearily up and was going away to bed without a good-night — custom now — but she stopped near the letter and eyed it awhile with a dead interest, then broke it open, and began to skim it over. Richards, sitting there with his chair tilted back against the wall and his chin between his knees, heard something fall. It was his wife. He sprang to her side, but she cried out:

"Leave me alone, I am too happy. Read the letter —

read it!"

He did. He devoured it, his brain reeling. The letter was from a distant State, and it said:

I am a stranger to you, but no matter: I have something to tell. I have just arrived home from Mexico, and learned about that episode. Of course you do not know who made that remark, but I know, and I am the only person living who does know. It was GOODSON. I knew him well, many years ago. I passed through your village that very night, and was his guest till the midnight train came along. I overheard him make that remark to the stranger in the dark — it was in Hale Alley. He and I talked of it the rest of the way home, and while smoking in his house. He mentioned many of your villagers in the course of his talk — most of them in a very uncomplimentary way, but two or three favorably: among these latter yourself. I say 'favorably'— nothing stronger. I remember his saying he did not actually LIKE any person in the town — not one; but that you — I THINK

*he said you — am almost sure, had done him a very great
service once, possibly without knowing the full value of it,
and he wished he had a fortune, he would leave it to you
when he died, and a curse apiece for the rest of the citizens.
Now, then, if it was you that did him that service, you are
his legitimate heir, and entitled to the sack of gold. I know
that I can trust to your honor and honesty, for in a citizen
of Hadleyburg these virtues are an unfailing inheritance,
and so I am going to reveal to you the remark, well satisfied
that if you are not the right man you will seek and find
the right one and see that poor Goodson's debt of gratitude
for the service referred to is paid. This is the remark: 'YOU
ARE FAR FROM BEING A BAD MAN: GO, AND
REFORM.'*

"HOWARD L. STEPHENSON"

"Oh, Edward, the money is ours, and I am so grateful,
oh, so grateful — kiss me, dear, it's forever since we kissed—

and we needed it so — the money — and now you are free of Pinkerton and his bank, and nobody's slave any more; it seems to me I could fly for joy."

It was a happy half hour that the couple spent there on the settee caressing each other; it was the old days come again — days that had begun with their courtship and lasted without a break till the stranger brought the deadly money. By-and-by the wife said:

"Oh, Edward, how lucky it was you did him that grand service, poor Goodson! I never liked him, but I love him now. And it was fine and beautiful of you never to mention it or brag about it." Then, with a touch of reproach, "But you ought to have told *me*, Edward, you ought to have told your wife, you know."

"Well, I — er — well, Mary, you see —"

"Now stop hemming and hawing, and tell me about it, Edward. I always loved you, and now I'm proud of you.

Everybody believes there was only one good generous soul in this village, and now it turns out that you — Edward, why don't you tell me?"

"Well — er — er — Why, Mary, I can't!"

"You *can't*? *Why* can't you?"

"You see, he — well, he — he made me promise I wouldn't."

The wife looked him over, and said, very slowly,

"Made — you — promise? Edward, what do you tell me that for?"

"Mary, do you think I would lie?"

She was troubled and silent for a moment, then she laid her hand within his and said:

"No...no. We have wandered far enough from our bearings — God spare us that! In all your life you have never uttered a lie. But now — now that the foundations of things seem to be crumbling from under us, we — we —" She lost her voice for a moment, then said, brokenly, "Lead us not into temptation. . . I think you made the promise, Edward. Let it rest so. Let us keep away from that ground. Now— that is all gone by; let us be happy again; it is no time for clouds."

Edward found it something of an effort to comply, for his mind kept wandering — trying to remember what the service was that he had done Goodson.

The couple lay awake the most of the night, Mary happy and busy, Edward busy, but not so happy. Mary was planning what she would do with the money. Edward was trying to recall that service. At first his conscience was sore on account of the lie he had told Mary — if it was a lie. After much reflection — suppose it *was* a lie? What then: Was it such a great matter? Aren't we *acting* lies? Then why not *tell* them? Look at Mary — look what she had done. While he was hurrying off on his honest errand, what was she doing? Lamenting because the papers hadn't been destroyed and the money kept! Is theft better than lying?

That point lost its sting — the lie dropped into the background and left comfort behind it. The next point came to the front: *had* he rendered that service? Well, here was Goodson's own evidence as reported in Stephenson's letter; there could be no better evidence than that — it was even *proof* that he had rendered it. Of course. So that point was settled...No, not quite. He recalled with a wince that this unknown Mr. Stephenson was just a trifle unsure as to whether the performer of it was Richards or some other— and, oh dear, he had to put Richards on his honor! He must himself decide wither that money must go — and Mr. Stephenson was not doubting that if he was the wrong man he would go honorably and find the right one. Oh, it was odious to put a man in such a situation — ah, why couldn't Stephenson have left out that doubt! What did he want to intrude that for?

Further reflection. How did it happen that *Richards'* name remained in Stephenson's mind as indicating the right man, and not some other man's name? That looked good. Yes, that looked very good. In fact, it went on looking better and better, straight along — until by-and-by it grew into positive *proof*. And then Richards put the matter at once out of his mind, for he had a private instinct that a proof once established is better left so.

He was feeling reasonably comfortable now, but there was still one other detail that kept pushing itself on his notice: of course he had done that service — that was settled; but what *was* that service? He must recall it — he would not go to sleep till he had recalled it; it would make his peace of mind perfect. And so he thought and thought. He thought of a dozen things — possible services, even probable services — but none of them seemed adequate, none of them seemed large enough, none of them seemed worth the money — worth the fortune Goodson had wished he could leave in his will. And besides, he couldn't remember having done them, anyway. Now, then — now, then — what *kind* of a service would it be that would make a man so inordinately grateful? Ah — the saving of his soul! That must be it. Yes, he could remember, now, how he once set himself the task of converting Goodson, and labored at it as much as — he was going to say three months; but upon closer examination it shrunk to a month, then to a week, then to a day, then to nothing. Yes, he remembered now, and with unwelcome vividness, that Goodson had told him to go to thunder and mind his own business — *he* wasn't hankering to follow Hadleyburg to heaven!

So that solution was a failure — he hadn't saved Goodson's soul. Richards was discouraged. Then after a little came another idea: had he saved Goodson's property? No, that wouldn't do — he hadn't any. His life? This is it! Of course. Why, he might have thought of it before. This time he was on the right track, sure. His imagination was hard at work in a minute, now.

Thereafter during a stretch of two exhausting hours he was busy saving Goodson's life. He saved it in all kinds of difficult and perilous ways. In every case he got it saved satisfactorily up to a certain point; then, just as he was beginning to get well persuaded that it had really happened, a troublesome detail would turn up which made the whole thing impossible. As in the matter of drowning, for instance. In that case he had swum out and tugged Goodson ashore in an unconscious state with a great crowd looking on and applauding, but when he had got it all thought out and was just beginning to remember all about it a whole swarm of disqualifying details arrived on the ground: the town would have known of it, it would glare like a limelight in his own memory instead of being an inconspicuous service which he had possibly rendered "without knowing its full value." And at this point he remembered that he couldn't swim, anyway.

Ah — *there* was a point which he had been overlooking from the start: it had to be a service which he had rendered "possibly without knowing the full value of it." Why, really, that ought to be an easy hunt — much easier than those others. And sure enough, by-and-by he found it. Goodson, years and years ago, came near marrying a very sweet and pretty girl, named Nancy Hewitt, but in some way or other the match had been broken off; the girl died, Goodson remained a bachelor, and by-and-by became a soured one and a frank despiser of the human species. Soon after the girl's death the village found out, or thought it had found out, that she carried a spoonful of negro blood in her veins. Richards worked at these details a good while, and in the end he thought he remembered things concerning them which must have gotten mislaid in his memory through long neglect. He seemed to dimly remember that it was *he* that found out about the negro blood; that it was he that told the village; that the village told Goodson where they got it; that he thus saved Goodson from marrying the tainted girl; that he had done him this great service "without knowing the full value of it," in fact without knowing that he *was* doing it; but that Goodson knew the value of it, and what a narrow escape he had had, and so went to his grave grateful to his benefactor and wishing he had a fortune to leave him. It was all clear and simple now, and the more he went over it the more luminous and certain it grew; and at last, when he nestled to sleep satisfied and happy, he remembered the whole thing just as if it had been yesterday. In fact, he dimly remembered Goodson's *telling* him his gratitude once. Meantime Mary had spent six thousand dollars on a new house for herself and a pair of slippers for her pastor, and then had fallen peacefully to rest.

That same Saturday evening the postman had delivered a letter to each of the other principal citizens — nineteen letters in all. No two of the envelopes were alike, and no two of the superscriptions were in the same hand, but the letters inside were just like each other in every detail but one. They were exact copies of the letter received by Richards — handwriting and all — and were all signed by Stephenson, but in place of Richards' name each receiver's own name appeared.

All night long eighteen principal citizens did what their caste-brother Richards was doing at the same time — they put in their energies trying to remember what notable service it was that they had unconsciously done Barclay Goodson. In no case was it a holiday job; still they succeeded.

And while they were at this work, which was difficult,

their wives put in the night spending the money, which was easy. During that one night the nineteen wives spent an average of seven thousand dollars each out of the forty thousand in the sack — a hundred and thirty-three thousand altogether.

Next day there was a surprise for Jack Halliday. He noticed that the faces of the nineteen chief citizens and their wives bore that expression of peaceful and holy happiness again. He could not understand it, neither was he able to invent any remarks about it that could damage it or disturb it. And so it was his turn to be dissatisfied with life. His private guesses at the reasons for the happiness failed in all instances, upon examination. When he met Mrs. Wilcox and noticed the placid ecstasy in her face, he said to himself, "Her cat has had kittens" — and went and asked the cook; it was not so; the cook had detected the happiness, but did not know the cause. When Halliday found the duplicate ecstasy in the face of "Shadbelly" Billson (village nickname), he was sure some neighbor of Billson's had broken his leg, but inquiry showed that this had not happened. The subdued ecstasy in Gregory Yates' face could mean but one thing — he was a mother-in-law short; it was another mistake. "And Pinkerton — Pinkerton — he has collected ten cents that he thought he was going to lose." And so on, and so on. In some cases the guesses had to remain in doubt, in the others they proved distinct errors. In the end Halliday said to himself, "Anyway, it foots up that there's nineteen Hadleyburg families temporarily in heaven: I don't know how it happened; I only know Providence is off duty today."

An architect and builder from the next State had lately ventured to set up a small business in this unpromising village, and his sign had now been hanging out a week. Not a customer yet; he was a discouraged man, and sorry he had come. But his weather changed suddenly now. First one and then another chief citizen's wife said to him privately:

"Come to my house Monday week — but say nothing about it for the present. We think of building."

He got eleven invitations that day. That night he wrote his daughter and broke off her match with her student. He said she could marry a mile higher than that.

Pinkerton the banker and two or three other well-to-do men planned country-seats — but waited. That kind don't count their chickens until they are hatched.

The Wilsons devised a grand new thing — a fancy-dress ball. They made no actual promises, but told all their acquaintanceship in confidence that they were thinking the matter over and thought they should give it — "and if we do, you will be invited, of course." People were surprised, and said, one to another, "Why, they are crazy, those poor

Wilsons, they can't afford it." Several among the nineteen said privately to their husbands, "It is a good idea, we will keep still till their cheap thing is over, then *we* will give one that will make it sick."

The days drifted along, and the bill of future squanderings rose higher and higher, wilder and wilder, more and more foolish and reckless. It began to look as if every member of the nineteen would not only spend his whole forty thousand dollars before receiving-day, but be actually in debt by the time he got the money. In some cases light-headed people did not stop with planning to spend, they really spent — on credit. They bought land, mortgages, farms, speculative stocks, fine clothes, horses, and various other things, paid down the bonus, and made themselves liable for the rest — at ten days. Presently the sober second thought came, and Halliday noticed that a ghastly anxiety was beginning to show up in a good many faces. Again he was puzzled, and didn't know what to make of it. "The Wilcox kittens aren't dead, for they weren't born; nobody's broken a leg; there's no shrinkage in mother-in-laws; *nothing* has happened — it is an insolvable mystery."

There was another puzzled man, too — the Rev. Mr. Burgess. For days, wherever he went, people seemed to follow him or to be watching out for him; and if he ever found himself in a retired spot, a member of the nineteen would be sure to appear, thrust an envelope privately into his hand, whisper "To be opened at the town-hall Friday evening," then vanish away like a guilty thing. He was expecting that there might be one claimant for the sack — doubtful, however, Goodson being dead — but it never occurred to him that all this crowd might be claimants. When the great Friday came at last, he found that he had nineteen envelopes.

Chapter 3

The town hall had never looked finer. The platform at the end of it was backed by a showy draping of flags; at intervals along the walls were festoons of flags; the gallery fronts were clothed in flags; the supporting columns were swathed in flags; all this was to impress the stranger, for he would be there in considerable force, and in a large degree he would be connected with the press. The house was full. The 412 fixed seats were occupied; also the 68 extra chairs which had been packed into the aisles; the steps of the platform were occupied; some distinguished strangers were given seats on the platform; at the horseshoe of tables which fenced the front and sides of the platform sat a strong force of special correspondents who had come from everywhere. It was the best-dressed house the town had ever produced. There were some tolerably expensive toilets there, and in several cases the ladies who wore them had the look of being unfamiliar with that kind of clothes. At least the town thought they had that look, but the notion could have arisen from the town's knowledge of the fact that these ladies had never inhabited such clothes before.

The gold-sack stood on a little table at the front of the platform where all the house could see it. The bulk of the house gazed at it with a burning interest, a mouth-watering interest, a wistful and pathetic interest; a minority of nineteen couples gazed at it tenderly, lovingly, proprietarily, and the male half of this minority kept saying over to themselves the moving little impromptu speeches of thankfulness for the audience's applause and congratulations which they were presently going to get up and deliver. Every now and then one of these got a piece of paper out of his vest pocket and privately glanced at it to refresh his memory.

Of course there was a buzz of conversation going on—there always is; but at last when the Rev. Mr. Burgess rose and laid his hand on the sack he could hear his microbes gnaw, the place was so still. He related the curious history of the sack, then went on to speak in warm terms of Hadleyburg's old and well-earned reputation for spotless honesty, and of the town's just pride in this reputation. He said that this reputation was a treasure of priceless value; that under Providence its value had now become inestimably enhanced, for the recent episode had spread this fame far and wide, and thus had focussed the eyes of the American world upon this village, and made its name for all time, as he hoped and believed, a synonym for commercial incorruptibility. [*Applause.*] "And who is to be the guardian of this noble treasure — the community as a whole? No! The responsibility is individual, not communal. From this day forth each and every one of you is in his own person its special guardian and individually responsible that no harm shall come to it. Do you — does each of you — accept this great trust? [*Tumultuous assent.*] Then all is well. Transmit it to your children and to your children's children. Today your purity is beyond reproach — see to it that it shall remain so. Today there is not a person in your community who could be beguiled to touch a penny not his own — see to it that you abide in this grace. [*"We will! we will!"*] This is not to make comparisons between ourselves and other communities — some of them ungracious toward us; they have their ways, we have ours; let us be content. [*Applause.*] I am done. Under my hand, my friends, rests a stranger's eloquent recognition of what we are: through him the world will always henceforth know what we are. We do not know who he is, but in your name I utter your gratitude, and ask you to raise your voices in endorsement."

The house rose in a body and made the walls quake with the thunders of its thankfulness for the space of a long minute. Then it sat down, and Mr. Burgess took an envelope out of his pocket. The house held its breath while he slit the envelope open and took from it a slip of paper. He read its contents — slowly and impressively — the audience listening with tranced attention to this magic document, each of whose words stood for an ingot of gold:

" 'The remark which I made to the distressed stranger was this: "You are very far from being a bad man; go, and reform." ' "

Then he continued: "We shall know in a moment now whether the remark here quoted corresponds with the one concealed in the sack; and if that shall prove to be so — and it undoubtedly will — this sack of gold belongs to a fellow-citizen who will henceforth stand before the nation as the symbol of the special virtue which had made our town famous throughout the land — Mr. Billson!"

The house had gotten itself all ready to burst into a proper tornado of applause; but instead of doing it, it seemed stricken with a paralysis; there was a deep hush for a moment or two, then a wave of whispered murmurs swept the place — of about this tenor: "*Billson!* oh, come, this is *too* thin! Twenty dollars to a stranger — or *anybody* — "*Billson!* Tell it to the marines!" And now at this point the house caught its breath all of a sudden in a new access of astonishment, for it discovered that whereas in one part of the hall Deacon Billson was standing up with his head meekly bowed, in another part of it Lawyer Wilson was doing the same. There was a wondering silence now for a while. Everybody was puzzled, and nineteen couples were surprised and indignant.

Billson and Wilson turned and stared at each other. Billson asked, bitingly,

"Why do *you* rise Mr. Wilson?"

"Because I have a right to. Perhaps you will be good enough to explain to the house why *you* rise?"

"With great pleasure. Because I wrote that paper."

It was Burgess' turn to be paralyzed. He stood looking vacantly at first one of the men and then the other, and did not seem to know what to do. The house was stupefied. Lawyer Wilson spoke up, now, and said.

"I ask the Chair to read the name signed to that paper."

That brought the Chair to itself, and it read out the name, "'John Wharton *Billson*.'"

"There!" shouted Billson, "what have you got to say for yourself, now? And what kind of apology are you going to make to me and to this insulted house for the imposture which you have attempted to pay here?"

"No apologies are due, sir; and as for the rest of it, I publicly charge you with pilfering my note from Mr. Burgess and substituting a copy of it signed with your own name. There is no other way by which you could have gotten hold of the test-remark; I alone, of living men, possessed the secret of its wording."

There was likely to be a scandalous state of things if this went on; everybody noticed with distress that the shorthand scribes were scribbling like mad; many people were crying "Chair, Chair! Order! order!" Burgess rapped with his gavel, and said:

"Let us not forget the proprieties due. There has evidently been a mistake somewhere, but surely that is all. If Mr. Wilson gave me an envelope — and I remembered now that he did — I still have it."

He took one out of his pocket, opened it, glanced at it, looked surprised and worried, and stood silent a few moments. Then he waved his hand in a wandering and mechanical way, and made an effort or two to say something, then gave it up, despondently. Several voices cried out:

"Read it! read it! What is it?"

So he began in a dazed and sleep-walker fashion:

" 'The remark which I made to the unhappy stranger was this:

You are far from being a bad man. [The house gazed at him marvelling.] Go, and reform." ' [Murmurs: "Amazing! what can this mean?"] "This one," said the Chair, "is signed Thurlow G. Wilson."

"There!" cried Wilson, "I reckon that settles it! I knew perfectly well my note was purloined."

"Purloined!" retorted Billson. "I'll let you know that neither you nor any man of your kidney must venture to —"

The Chair. "Order, gentlemen, order! Take your seats, both of you, please."

They obeyed, shaking their heads and grumbling angrily. The house was profoundly puzzled; it did not know what to do with this curious emergency. Presently Thompson got up. Thompson was the hatter. He would have liked to be a Nineteener; but such was not for him; his stock of hats was not considerable enough for the position. He said:

"Mr. Chairman, if I may be permitted to make a suggestion, can both of these gentlemen be right? I put it to you, sir, can both have happened to say the very same words to the stranger? It seems to me —"

The tanner got up and interrupted him. The tanner was a disgruntled man; he believed himself entitled to be a Nineteener, but he couldn't get recognition. It made him a little unpleasant in his ways and speech. Said he:

"Sho, *that's* not the point! *That* could happen — twice in a hundred years — but the other thing. *Neither* of them gave the twenty dollars!" [*A ripple of applause.*]

Billson. "I did!"

Wilson. "I did!"

Then each accused the other of pilfering.

The Chair. "Order! Sit down, if you please — both of you. Neither of the notes has been out of my possession at any moment."

A Voice. "Good — that settles *that!*"

The Tanner. "Mr. Chairman, one thing is now plain: one of these men has been eavesdropping under the other one's bed, and filching family secrets. If it is not unparliamentary to suggest it, I will remark that both are equal to it. [*The Chair.* "Order! order!"] I withdraw the remark, sir, and will confine myself to suggesting that *if* one of them has overheard the other reveal the test-remark to his wife, we shall catch him now."

A Voice. "How?"

The Tanner. "Easily. The two have not quoted the remark in exactly the same words. You would have noticed that, if there hadn't been a considerable stretch of time and an exciting quarrel inserted between the two readings."

A Voice. "Name the difference."

The Tanner. "The word *very* is in Billson's note, and not in the other."

Many Voices. "That's so — he's right."

The Tanner. "And so, if the Chair will examine the test-remark in the sack, we shall know which of these two frauds — [*The Chair.* "Order!"] — which of these two adventurers — [*The Chair.* "Order! order!"] — which of these two gentlemen — [*laughter and applause*] — is entitled to wear the belt as being the first dishonest blatherskite ever bred in this town — which he has dishonored, and which will be a sultry place for him from now out!" [*Vigorous applause.*]

Many Voices. "Open it! — open the sack!"

Mr. Burgess made a slit in the sack, slid his hand in and brought out an envelope. In it were a couple of folded notes. He said:

"One of these is marked, 'Not to be examined until all written communications which have been addressed to the Chair — if any — shall have been read.' The other is marked *The Test.*' Allow me. It is worded — to wit:

" 'I do not require that the first half of the remark which was made to me by my benefactor shall be quoted with exactness, for it was not striking, and could be forgotten; but its closing fifteen words are quite striking, and I think easily rememberable; unless *these* shall be accurately reproduced, let the applicant be regarded as an imposter. My benefactor began by saying he seldom gave advice to any one, but that it always bore the hall-mark of high value when he did give it. Then he said this — and it has never faded from my memory: *"You are far from being a bad man —"'* "

Fifty Voices. "That settles it — the money's Wilson's! Wilson! Wilson! Speech! Speech!"

People jumped up and crowded around Wilson, wringing his hand and congratulating fervently — meantime the Chair was hammering with the gavel and shouting:

"Order, gentlemen! Order! Order! Let me finish reading, please." When quiet was restored, the reading was resumed — as follows:

" ' "Go, and reform — or, mark my words — some day, for your sins, you will die and go to hell or Hadleyburg — TRY AND MAKE IT THE FORMER." ' "

A ghastly silence followed. First an angry cloud began to settle darkly upon the faces of the citizenship; after a pause the cloud began to rise, and a tickled expression tried to take its place; tried so hard that it was only kept under with great and painful difficulty; the reporters, the Brixtonites, and other strangers bent their heads down and shielded their faces with their hands, and managed to hold in by main strength and heroic courtesy. At this most inopportune time burst upon the stillness the roar of a solitary voice — Jack Halliday's:

"That's got the hall-mark on it!"

Then the house let go, strangers and all. Even Mr. Burgess' gravity broke down presently, then the audience considered itself officially absolved from all restraint, and it made the most of its privilege. It was a good long laugh, and a tempestuously wholehearted one, but it ceased at last — long enough for Mr. Burgess to try to resume, and for the people to get their eyes partially wiped; then it broke out again; and afterward yet again; then at last Burgess was able to get out these serious words:

"It is useless to try to disguise the fact — we find ourselves in the presence of a matter of grave import. It involves the honor of your town, it strikes at the town's good name. The difference of a single word between the test-remarks offered by Mr. Wilson and Mr. Billson was itself a serious thing, since it indicated that one or the other of these gentlemen had committed a theft —"

The two men were sitting limp, nerveless, crushed; but at these words both were electrified into movement, and started to get up —

"Sit down!" said the Chair, sharply, and they obeyed. "That, as I have said, was a serious thing. And it was — but for only one of them. But the matter has become graver; for the honor of *both* is now in formidable peril. Shall I go even further, and say in inextricable peril? *Both* left out the crucial fifteen words." He paused. During several moments he allowed the pervading stillness to gather and deepen its impressive effects, then added: "There would seem to be but one way whereby this could happen. I ask these gentlemen — Was there *collusion? — agreement?*"

A low murmur sifted through the house; its import was, "He's got them both."

Billson was not used to emergencies; he sat in a helpless collapse. But Wilson was a lawyer. He struggled to his feet, pale and worried, and said:

"I ask the indulgence of the house while I explain this most painful matter. I am sorry to say what I am about to say, since it must inflict irreparable injury upon Mr. Billson, whom I have always esteemed and respected until now, and in whose invulnerability to temptation I entirely believed — as did you all. But for the preservation of my own honor I must speak — and with frankness. I confess with shame — and I now beseech your pardon for it — that I said to the ruined stranger all of the words contained in the test-remark, including the disparaging fifteen. [*Sensation.*] When the late publication was made I recalled them, and I resolved to claim the sack of coin, for by every right I was entitled to it. Now I will ask you to consider this point, and weigh it well: that stranger's gratitude to me that night knew no bounds; he said himself that he could find no words for it that were adequate, and that if he should ever be able he would repay me a thousandfold. Now, then, I ask you this: could I expect — could I believe — could I even remotely imagine — that, feeling as he did, he would do so ungrateful a thing as to add those quite unnecessary fifteen words to his test? — set a trap for me? — expose me as a slanderer of my own town before my own people assembled in a public hall? It was preposterous; it was impossible. His test would contain only the kindly opening clause of my remark. Of that I had no shadow of doubt. You would have thought as I did. You would not have expected a base betrayal from one whom you had befriended and against whom you had committed no offense. And so, with perfect confidence, perfect trust, I wrote on a piece of paper the opening words— ending with 'Go, and reform,' — and signed it. When I was about to put it in an envelope I was called into my back office, and without thinking I left the paper lying open on my desk." He stopped, turned his head slowly toward Billson, waited a moment, then added: "I ask you to note this: when I returned, a little later, Mr. Billson was retiring by my street door." [*Sensation.*]

In a moment Billson was on his feet and shouting:

"It's a lie! It's an infamous lie!"

The Chair. "Be seated, sir! Mr. Wilson has the floor."

Billson's friends pulled him into his seat and quieted him, and Wilson went on:

"Those are the simple facts. My note was now lying in a different place on the table from where I had left it. I noticed that, but attached no importance to it, thinking a draught had blown it there. That Mr. Billson would read a private paper was a thing which could not occur to me; he was an honorable man, and he would be above that. If you will allow me to say it, I think his extra word '*very*'

THE MAN THAT CORRUPTED HADLEYBURG

stands explained; it is attributable to a defect of memory. I was the only man in the world who could furnish here any detail of the test-mark — by *honorable* means. I have finished."

There is nothing in the world like a persuasive speech to fuddle the mental apparatus and upset the convictions and debauch the emotions of an audience not practiced in the tricks and delusions of oratory. Wilson sat down victorious. The house submerged him in tides of approving applause; friends swarmed to him and shook him by the hand and congratulated him, and Billson was shouted down and not allowed to say a word. The Chair hammered and hammered with its gavel, and kept shouting:

"But let us proceed, gentlemen, let us proceed!"

At last there was a measurable degree of quiet, and the hatter said:

"But what is there to proceed with, sir, but to deliver

the money?"

Voices. "That's it! That's it! Come forward, Wilson!"

The Hatter. "I move three cheers for Mr. Wilson, Symbol of the special virtue which —"

The cheers burst forth before he could finish; and in the midst of them — and in the midst of the clamor of the gavel also — some enthusiasts mounted Wilson on a big friend's shoulder and were going to fetch him in triumph to the platform. The Chair's voice now rose above the noise —

"Order! To your places! You forget that there is still a document to be read." When quiet had been restored he took up the document, and was going to read it, but laid it down again, saying, "I forgot; this is not to be read until all written communications received by me have first been read." He took an envelope out of his pocket, removed its enclosure, glanced at it — seemed astonished — held it out and gazed at it — stared at it.

Twenty or thirty voices cried out:

"What is it? Read it! read it!"

And he did — slowly, and wondering:

" 'The remark which I made to the stranger — [*Voices.* "Hello! how's this?"] — was this: "You are far from being a bad man. [*Voices.* "Great Scott!"] Go, and reform." ' [*Voice.* "Oh, saw my leg off!"] Signed by Mr. Pinkerton the banker."

The pandemonium of delight which turned itself loose now was a sort to make the judicious weep. Those whose withers were unwrung laughed till the tears ran down; the reporters, in throes of laughter, set down disordered pot-hooks which would never in the world be decipherable; and a sleeping dog jumped up, scared out of its wits, and barked itself crazy at the turmoil. All manner of cries were scattered through the din: "We're getting rich — *two* Symbols

of Incorruptibility! — without counting Billson!" "*Three!* —
count Shadbelly in — we can't have too many!" "All right—
Billson's elected!" Alas, poor Wilson — victim of *two*
thieves!"

A Powerful Voice. "Silence! The Chair's fished up
something more out of its pocket."

Voices. "Hurrah! Is it something fresh; Read it! read!
read!"

The Chair [reading]. "'The remark which I made,' etc.
'You are far from being a bad man. Go,' etc. Signed,
'Gregory Yates.'"

Tornado of Voices. "Four Symbols!" "Rah for Yates!"
"Fish again!"

The house was in a roaring humor now, and ready to
get all the fun out of the occasion that might be in it. Several
Nineteeners, looking pale and distressed, got up and began
to work their way toward the aisles, but a score of shouts

went up:

"The doors, the doors — close the doors; no Incorruptible shall leave this place! Sit down, everybody!"

The mandate was obeyed.

"Fish again! Read! read!"

The Chair fished again, and once more the familiar words began to fall from its lips — " 'You are far from being a bad man —' "

"Name! name! What's his name?"

" 'L. Ingoldsby Sargent.' "

"Five elected! Pile up the Symbols! Go on, go on!"

" 'You are far from being a bad —' "

"Name! name!"

" 'Nicholas Whitworth.' "

"Hooray! hooray! it's a symbolical day!"

Somebody wailed in, and began to sing this rhyme (leaving out "it's") to the lovely "Mikado" tune of "When a man's afraid, a beautiful maid —"; the audience joined in, with joy, then, just in time, somebody contributed another line —

"And don't you this forget —"

The house roared it out. A third line was at once furnished—

"Corruptibles far from Hadleyburg are —"

The house roard that one too. As the last note died, Jack Halliday's voice rose high and clear, freighted with a final line —

"But the Symbols are here, you bet!"

That was sung, with booming enthusiasm. Then the happy house started in at the beginning and sang the four lines through twice, with immense swing and dash, and finished up with a crashing three-times-three and a tiger for "Hadleyburg the Incorruptible and all Symbols of it which we shall find worthy to receive the hall-mark tonight."

Then the shoutings at the Chair began again, all over

the place:

"Go on! go on! Read! read some more! Read all you've got!"

"That's it — go on! We are winning eternal celebrity!"

A dozen men got up now and began to protest. They said that this farce was the work of some abandoned joker, and was an insult to the whole community. Without a doubt these signatures were all forgeries — "Sit down! sit down! Shut up! You are confessing. We'll find *your* names in the lot."

"Mr. Chairman, how many of those envelopes have you got?"

The Chair counted.

"Together with those that have been already examined, there are nineteen."

A storm of derisive applause broke out.

"Perhaps they all contain the secret. I move that you

open them all and read every signature that is attached to
a note of that sort — and read also the first eight words
of the note."

"Second the motion!"

It was put and carried — uproariously. Then poor old
Richards got up, and his wife rose and stood at his side.
Her head was bent down, so that none might see that she
was crying. Her husband gave her his arm, and so supporting her, he began to speak in a quavering voice:

"My friends, you have known us two — Mary and me—
all our lives, and I think you have liked us and respected
us —"

The Chair interrupted him:

"Allow me. It is quite true — that which you are saying, Mr. Richards; this town *does* know you two; it *does* like
you; it *does* respect you; more — it honors you and *loves*
you —"

Halliday's voice rang out:

"That's the hall-marked truth, too! If the Chair is right, let the house speak up and say it. Rise! Now, then — hip! hip! hip! — all together!"

The house rose in mass, faced toward the old couple eagerly, filled the air with a snowstorm of waving hand-kerchiefs, and delivered the cheers with all its affectionate heart.

The Chair then continued:

"What I was going to say is this: We know your good heart, Mr. Richards, but this is not a time for the exercise of charity toward offenders. [Shouts of "Right! right!"] I see your generous purpose in your face, but I cannot allow you to plead for these men —"

"But I was going to —"

"Please take your seat, Mr. Richards. We must examine the rest of these notes — simple fairness to the men who

have already been exposed requires this. As soon as that
has been done — I give you my word for this — you shall
be heard."

Many Voices. "Right! — the Chair is right — no inter-
ruption can be permitted at this state! Go on! — the names!
the names! — according to the terms of the motion!"

The old couple sat reluctantly down, and the husband
whispered to the wife, "It is pitifully hard to have to wait;
the shame will be greater than ever when they find we were
only going to plead for *ourselves.*"

Straightway the jollity broke loose again with the
reading of the names.

" 'You are far from being a bad man —' Signature,
'Robert J. Titmarsh.'

" 'You are far from being a bad man —' Signature,
'Eliphalet Weeks.'

" 'You are far from being a bad man —' Signature, Oscar

B. Wilder.'"

At this point the house lit upon the idea of taking the eight words out of the Chairman's hands. He was not un-thankful for that. Thenceforward he held up each note in its turn, and waited. The house droned out the eight words in a massed and measured and musical deep volume of sound (with a daringly close resemblance to a well-known church chant) — "'You are f-a-r from being a b-a-a-a-d man.'" Then the Chair said, "Signature, 'Archibald Wilcox.'" And so on, and so on, name after name, and everybody had an increasingly and gloriously good time except the wretched Nineteen. Now and then, when a particularly shining name was called, the house made the Chair wait while it chanted the whole of the test-remark from the beginning to the clos-ing words, "And go to hell or Hadleyburg — try and make it the for-or-m-e-r!" And in these special cases they added a grand and agonized and imposing "A-a-a-a-men!"

The list dwindled, dwindled, dwindled, poor old
Richards keeping tally of the count, wincing when a name
resembling his own was pronounced, and waiting in
miserable suspense for the time to come when it would be
his humiliating privilege to rise with Mary and finish his
plea, which he was intending to word thus: "...for until
now we have never done any wrong thing, but have gone
our humble way unreproached. We are very poor, we are
old, and have no chick nor child to help us; we were sorely
tempted, and we fell. It was my purpose when I got up before
to make confession and beg that my name might not be
read out in this public place, for it seemed to us that we
could not bear it; but I was prevented. It was just; it was
our place to suffer with the rest. It has been hard for us.
It is the first time we have ever heard our name fall from
any one's lips — sullied. Be merciful — for the sake of the
better days; make our shame as light to bear as in your chari-

ty you can." At this point in his revery Mary nudged him, perceiving that his mind was absent. The house was chanting. "You are f-a-r," etc.

"Be ready," Mary whispered. "Your name comes now; he has read eighteen."

The chant ended.

"Next! next! next!" came volleying from all over the house.

Burgess put his hand into his pocket. The old couple, trembling, began to rise, Burgess fumbled a moment, then said,

"I find I have read them all."

Faint with joy and surprise, the couple sank into their seats, and Mary whispered:

"Oh, bless God, we are saved! — he has lost ours — I wouldn't give this for a hundred of those sacks!"

The house burst out with its "Mikado" travesty, and

sang it three times with ever-increasing enthusiasm, rising
to its feet when it reached for the third time the closing
line —

"But the Symbols are here, you bet!"
and finishing up with cheers and a tiger for "Hadleyburg
purity and our eighteen immortal respresentatives of it."

Then Wingate, the saddler, got up and proposed cheers
"for the cleanest man in town, the one solitary important
citizen in it who didn't try to steal that money — Edward
Richards."

They were given with great and moving heartiness; then
somebody proposed that Richards be elected sole Guardian
and Symbol of the now Sacred Hadleyburg Tradition, with
power and right to stand up and look the whole sarcastic
world in the face.

Passed, by acclamation; then they sang the "Mikado"
again, and ended it with,

"And there's *one* Symbol left, you bet!"

There was a pause; then —

A Voice. "Now, then, who's to get the sack?"

The Tanner (with bitter sarcasm). "That's easy. The money has to be divided among the eighteen Incorruptibles. They gave the suffering stranger twenty dollars apiece — and that remark — each in his turn — it took twenty-two minutes for the procession to move past. Staked the stranger — total contribution, $360. All they want is just the loan back — and interest — forty thousand dollars altogether."

Many voices [derisively]. That's it! Divvy! divvy! Be kind to the poor — don't keep them waiting!"

The Chair. "Order! I now offer the stranger's remaining document. It says: 'If no claimant shall appear [*grand chorus of groans*], I desire that you open the sack and count out the money to the principal citizens of your town, they to take it in trust [*Cries of "Oh! Oh! Oh!"*], and use it in

such ways as to them shall seem best for the propagation
and preservation of your community's noble reputation for
incorruptible honesty [*more cries*] — a reputation to which
their names and their efforts will add a new and far-reaching
lustre.' [*Enthusiastic outburst of sarcastic applause.*] That seems
to be all. No — here is a postscript:

"'P.S. — CITIZENS OF HADLEYBURG: There *is* no
test-remark — nobody made one. [*Great sensation.*] There
wasn't any pauper stranger, nor any twenty-dollar contribution, nor any accompanying benediction and compliment—
these are all inventions. [*General buzz and hum of astonishment and delight.*] Allow me to tell my story — it will take
but a word or two. I passed through your town at a certain time, and received a deep offense which I had not
earned. Any other man would have been content to kill
one or two of you and call it square, but to me that would
have been a trivial revenge, and inadequate; for the dead

do not *suffer*. Besides, I could not kill you all — and, anyway, made as I am, even that would not have satisfied me. I wanted to damage every man in the place, and every woman — and not in their bodies or in their estate, but in their vanity — the place where feeble and foolish people are most vulnerable. So I disguised myself and came back and studied you. You were easy game. You had an old and lofty reputation for honesty, and naturally you were proud of it — it was your treasure of treasures, the very apple of your eye. As soon as I found out that you carefully and vigilantly kept yourselves and your children *out of temptation*, I knew how to proceed. Why, you simple creatures, the weakest of all weak things is a virtue which has not been tested in the fire. I laid a plan, and gathered a list of names. My project was to corrupt Hadleyburg the incorruptible. My idea was to make liars and thieves of nearly half a hundred smirchless men and women who had never in their

lives uttered a lie or stolen a penny. I was afraid of Goodson. He was neither born nor reared in Hadleyburg. I was
afraid that if I started to operate my scheme by getting my
letter laid before you, you would say to yourselves, "Goodson is the only man among us who would give away twenty dollars to a poor devil" — and then you might not bite
at my bait. But Heaven took Goodson; then I knew I was
safe, and I set my trap and baited it. It may be that I shall
not catch all the men to whom I mailed the pretended test
secret, but I shall catch the most of them, if I know
Hadleyburg nature. [*Voices.* "Right — he got every last one
of them."] I believe they will even steal ostensible *gamble-*
money, rather than miss, poor, tempted, and mistrained
fellows. I am hoping to eternally and everlastingly squelch
your vanity and give Hadleyburg a new renown — one that
will *stick* — and spread far. If I have succeeded, open the
sack and summon the Committee on Propagation and

Preservation of the Hadleyburg Reputation.'"

A Cyclone of Voices. "Open it! Open it! The Eighteen to the front! Committee on Propagation of the Tradition! Forward — the Incorruptibles!"

The Chair ripped the sack wide, and gathered up a handful of bright, broad, yellow coins, shook them together, then examined them —

"Friends, they are only gilded disks of lead!"

There was a crashing outbreak of delight over this news, and when the noise had subsided, the tanner called out:

"By right of apparent seniority in this business, Mr. Wilson is Chairman of the Committee on Propagation of the Tradition. I suggest that he step forward on behalf of his pals, and receive in trust the money."

A Hundred Voices. "Wilson! Wilson! Wilson! Speech! Speech!"

Wilson [*in a voice trembling with anger*]. "You will allow me to say, without apologies for my language, *damn* the money!"

A Voice. "Oh, and him a Baptist!"

A Voice. "Seventeen Symbols left! Step up, gentlemen, and assume your trust!"

There was a pause — no response.

The Saddler. "Mr. Chairman, we've got *one* clean man left, anyway, out of the late aristocracy; and he needs money, and deserves it. I move that you appoint Jack Halliday to get up there and auction off that sack of gilt twenty dollar pieces, and give the result to the right man — the man whom Hadleyburg delights to honor — Edward Richards."

This was received with great enthusiasm, the dog taking a hand again; the saddler started the bids at a dollar, the Brixton folk and Barnum's representative fought hard for it, the people cheered every jump that the bids made, the excitement climbed moment by moment higher and

higher, the bidders got on their mettle and grew steadily
more and more daring, more and more determined, the
jumps went from a dollar up to five, then to ten, then to
twenty, then fifty, then to a hundred, then —

At the beginning of the auction Richards whispered in
distress to his wife: "Oh, Mary, can we allow it? It —
it — you see, it is an honor-reward, a testimonial to purity
of character, and — and — can we allow it? Hadn't I better
get up and — Oh, Mary, what ought we to do? — what
do you think we —" [*Halliday's voice. "Fifteen I'm bid! —
fifteen for the sack! — twenty! — ah, thanks! — thirty — thanks
again! Thirty, thirty, thirty! do I hear forty? — forty it is! Keep
the ball rolling, gentlemen, keep it rolling! — fifty! — thanks,
noble Roman! — going at fifty, fifty, fifty! — seventy! ninety!—
splendid! — a hundred! — pile it up, pile it up! — hundred and
twenty — forty! — just in time! — hundred and fifty! — TWO
hundred! — superb! Do I hear two h — thanks! — two hundred*

and fifty! —"]

"It is another temptation, Edward — I'm all in a tremble — but, oh, we've escaped *one* temptation, and that ought
to warn us, to — ["*Six did I hear? — thanks! — six fifty, six
f — SEVEN hundred!*"] And yet, Edward, when you think—
nobody susp — ["*Eight hundred dollars! — hurrah! — make
it nine! — Mr. Parsons, did I hear you say — thanks! — nine—
this noble sack of virgin lead going at only nine hundred dollars,
gilding and all — come! do I hear — a thousand! — gratefully
yours! — did some one say eleven? — a sack which is going to
be the most celebrated in the whole Uni —*"] "Oh, Edward"
(*beginning to sob*), "we are *so* poor! — but — but — do as
you think best — do as you think best."

Edward fell — that is, he sat still; sat with a conscience
which was not satisfied, but which was overpowered by
circumstances.

Meanwhile a stranger, who looked like an amateur

detective gotten up as an impossible English earl, had been watching the evening's proceedings with manifest interest, and with a contented expression in his face; and he had been privately commenting to himself. He was now soliloquizing somewhat like this: "None of the Eighteen are bidding; that is not satisfactory; I must change that — the dramatic unities require it; they must buy the sack they tried to steal; they must pay a heavy price, too — some of them are rich. And other thing, when I make a mistake in Hadleyburg nature the man that puts that error upon me is entitled to a high honorarium, and some one must pay it. This poor old Richards has brought my judgment to shame; he is an honest man; — I don't understand it, but I acknowledge it. Yes, he saw my deuces — *and* with a straight flush, and by rights the pot is his. And it shall be a jackpot, too, if I can manage it. He disappointed me, but let that pass."

He was watching the bidding. At a thousand, the

market broke; the prices tumbled swiftly. He waited — and
still watched. One competitor dropped out; then another,
and another. He put in a bid or two, now. When the bids
had sunk to ten dollars, he added a five; some one raised
him a three; he waited a moment, then flung in a fifty-dollar
jump, and the sack was his — at $1,282. The house broke
out in cheers — then stopped; for he was on his feet and
had lifted his hand. He began to speak.

"I desire to say a word, and ask a favor. I am a speculator in rarities, and I have dealings with persons interested
in numismatics all over the world. I can make a profit on
this purchase, just as it stands; but there is a way, if I can
get your approval, whereby I can make every one of these
leaden twenty dollar pieces worth its face in gold, and
perhaps more. Grant me that approval, and I will give part
of my gains to your Mr. Richards, who invulnerable probity you have so justly and so cordially recognized tonight;

his share shall be ten thousand dollars, and I will hand him the money tomorrow. [*Great applause from the house.* But the "invulnerable probity" made the Richardses blush prettily; however, it went for modesty, and did no harm.] If you will pass my proposition by a good majority — I would like a two-thrids vote — I will regard that as the town's consent, and that is all I ask. Rarities are always helped by any device which will rouse curiosity and compel remark. Now if I may have your permission to stamp upon the faces of each of these ostensible coins the names of the eighteen gentlemen who —"

Nine-tenths of the audience were on their feet in a moment — dog and all — and the proposition was carried with a whirlwind of approving applause and laughter.

They sat down, and all the Symbols except "Dr." Clay Harkness got up, violently protesting against the proposed outrage, and threatening to —

"I beg you not to threaten me," said the stranger, calmly. "I know my legal rights, and am not accustomed to being frightened at bluster." [*Applause.*] He sat down. "Dr." Harkness saw an opportunity here. He was one of the two very rich men of the place, and Pinkerton was the other. Harkness was proprietor of a mint; that is to say, a popular patent medicine. He was running for the Legislature on one ticket, and Pinkerton on the other. It was a close race and a hot one, and getting hotter every day. Both had strong appetites for money; each had bought a great tract of land, with a purpose; there was going to be a new railway, and each wanted to be in the Legislature and help locate the route to his own advantage; a single vote might make the decision, and with it two or three fortunes. The stake was large, and Harkness was a daring speculator. He was sitting close to the stranger. He leaned over while one or another of the other Symbols was entertaining the house with protests and appeals, and asked in a whisper,

"What is your price for the sack?"

"Forty thousand dollars."

"I'll give you twenty."

"No."

"Twenty-five."

"No."

"Say thirty."

"The price is forty thousand dollars; not a penny less."

"All right, I'll give it. I will come to the hotel at ten in the morning. I don't want it known; will see you privately."

"Very good." Then the stranger got up and said to the house:

"I find it late. The speeches of these gentlemen are not without merit, not without interest, not without grace; yet if I may be excused I will take my leave. I thank you for petition. I ask the Chair to keep the sack for me until tomorrow, and to hand these three five-hundred-dollar notes to Mr. Richards." They were passed up to the Chair. "At nine I will call for the sack, and at eleven will deliver the rest of the ten thousand to Mr. Richards in person, at his home. Good night."

Then he slipped out, and left the audience making a vast noise, which was composed of a mixture of cheers, the "Mikado" song, dog-disapproval, and the chant, "you are f-a-r from being a b-a-a-d man — a-a-a-a-men!"

Chapter 4

At home the Richardses had to endure congratulations and compliments until midnight. Then they were left to themselves. They looked a little sad, and they sat silent and thinking. Finally Mary sighed and said,

"Do you think we are to blame, Edward — *much* to blame?" and her eyes wandered to the accusing triplet of big bank-notes lying on the table, where the congratulators had been gloating over them and reverently fingering them. Edward did not answer at once; then he brought out a sigh and said, hesitatingly:

"We — we couldn't help it, Mary. It — well, it was ordered. *All* things are."

Mary glanced up and looked at him steadily, but he

didn't return the look. Presently she said:

"I thought congratulations and praises always tasted good. But — it seems to me, now — Edward?"

"Well?"

"Are you going to stay in the bank?"

"N-no."

"Resign?"

"In the morning — by note."

"It does seem best."

Richards bowed his head in his hands and muttered:

"Before, I was not afraid to let oceans of people's money pour through my hands, but — Mary, I am so tired, so tired —"

"We will go to bed."

At nine in the morning the stranger called for the sack and took it to the hotel in a cab. At ten Harkness had a talk with him privately. The stranger asked for and got five

checks on a metropolitan bank — drawn to "Bearer," —
four for $1,500 each, and one for $34,000. He put one of
the former in his pocket-book, and the remainder, representing $38,500, he put in an envelope, and with these he
added a note, which he wrote after Harkness was gone. At
eleven he called at the Richards' house and knocked. Mrs.
Richards peeped through the shutters, then went and received the envelope, and the stranger disappeared without a
word. She came back flushed and a little unsteady on her
legs, and gasped out:

"I am sure I recognized him! Last night it seemed to
me that maybe I had seen him somewhere before."

"He is the man that brought the sack here?"

"I am almost sure of it."

"Then he is the ostensible Stephenson too, and sold
every important citizen in this town with his bogus secret.
Now if he has sent checks instead of money, we are sold

too, after we thought we had escaped. I was beginning to feel fairly comfortable once more, after my night's rest, but the look of that envelope makes me sick. It isn't fat enough; $8,500 in even the largest bank-notes makes more bulk than that."

"Edward, why do you object to checks?"

"Checks signed by Stephenson! I am resigned to take the $8,500 if it could come in bank-notes — for it does seem that it was so ordered, Mary — but I have never had much courage, and I have not the pluck to try to market a check signed with that disastrous name. It would be a trap. That man tried to catch me; we escaped somehow or other; and now he is trying a new way. If it is checks —"

"Oh, Edward, it is *too* bad!" and she held up the checks and began to cry.

"Put them in the fire! quick! we mustn't be tempted. It is a trick to make the world laugh at *us*, along with the rest, and — Give them to *me*, since you can't do it!" He snatched them and tried to hold his grip till he could get to the stove; but he was human, and he was a cashier, and he stopped a moment to make sure of the signature. Then he came near to fainting.

"Fan me, Mary, fan me! They are the same as gold!"

"Oh, how lovely, Edward! Why?"

"Signed by Harkness. What can the mystery of that be, Mary?"

"Edward, do you think —"

"Look here — look at this! Fifteen — fifteen — fifteen— thirty-four. Thirty-eight thousand five hundred! Mary, the sack isn't worth twelve dollars, and Harkness — apparently — has paid about par for it."

"And does it all come to us, do you think — instead of the ten thousand?"

"Why, it looks like it. And the checks are made to

'Bearer,' too."

"Is that good, Edward? What is it for?"

"A hint to collect them at some distant bank, I reckon. Perhaps Harkness doesn't want the matter known. What is that — a note?

"Yes, It was with the checks."

It was in the "Stephenson" handwriting, but there was no signature. It said:

"*I am a disappointed man. Your honesty is beyond the reach of temptation. I had a different idea about it, but I wronged you in that, and I beg pardon, and do it sincerely. I honor you — and that is sincere, too. This town is not worthy to kiss the hem of your garment. Dear sir, I made a square bet with myself that there were nineteen debauchable men in your self-righteous community. I have lost. Take the whole pot, you are entitled to it.*"

Richards drew a deep sigh, and said:

"It seems written with fire — it burns so. Mary — I am miserable again."

"I, too. Ah, dear, I wish —"

"To think, Mary — he *believes* in me."

"Oh, don't Edward — I can't bear it."

"If those beautiful words were deserved, Mary — and God knows I believed I deserved them once — I think I could give the forty thousand dollars for them. And I would put that paper away, as representing more than gold and jewels, and keep it always. But now — We could not live in the shadow of its accusing presence, Mary."

He put it in the fire.

A messenger arrived and delivered an envelope. Richards took from it a note and read it; it was from Burgess:

"You saved me, in a difficult time. I saved you last night. It was at cost of a lie, but I made the sacrifice freely, and out of grateful heart. None in this village knows so well as I know

how brave and good and noble you are. At bottom you cannot respect me, knowing as you do of that matter of which I am accused, and by the general voice condemned; but I beg that you will at least believe that I am a grateful man; it will help me to bear my burden.

[Signed] "BURGESS."

"Saved, once more. And on such terms!" He put the note in the fire. "I — I wish I were dead, Mary, I wish I were out of it all."

"Oh, these are bitter, bitter days, Edward. The stabs, through their very generosity, are so deep — and they come so fast!"

Three days before the election each of two thousand voters suddenly found himself in possession of a prized memento — one of the renowned bogus double-eagles. Around one of its faces was stamped these words "THE RE-MARK I MADE TO THE POOR STRANGER WAS —"

Around the other face was stamped these: "GO, AND REFORM. [SIGNED] PINKERTON." Thus the entire remaining refuse of the renowned joke was emptied upon a single head, and with calamitous effect. It revived the recent vast laugh and concentrated it upon Pinkerton; and Harkness' election was a walk-over.

Within twenty-four hours after the Richardses had received their checks their consciences were quieting down, discouraged; the old couple were learning to reconcile themselves to the sin which they had committed. But they were to learn, now, that a sin takes on new and real terrors when there seems a chance that it is going to be found out. This gives it a fresh and most substantial and important aspect. At church the morning sermon was of the usual pattern; it was the same old things said in the same old way; they had heard them a thousand times and found them innocuous, next to meaningless, and easy to sleep under; but now it was different: the sermon seemed to bristle with accusations; it seemed aimed straight and specially at people who were concealing deadly sins. After church they got away from the mob of congratulators as soon as they could, and hurried homeward, chilled to the bone at they did not know what — vague, shadowy, indefinite fears. And by chance they caught a glimpse of Mr. Burgess as he turned a corner. He paid no attention to their nod of recognition! He hadn't seen it; but they did not know that. What could his conduct mean? It might mean — it might mean — oh, a dozen dreadful things. Was it possible that he knew that Richards could have cleared him of guilt in that bygone time, and had been silently waiting for a chance to even up accounts? At home, in their distress they got to imagining that their servent might have been in the next room listening when Richards revealed the secret to his wife that he knew of Burgess' innocence; next, Richards began to imagine that he had heard the swish of a gown in there at that time; next, he was sure he *had* heard it. They would call Sarah in, on a pretext, and watch her face: if she had been betraying them to Mr. Burgess, it would show in her manner. They asked her some questions — questions which were so random and incoherent and seemingly purposeless that the girl felt sure that the old people's mind had been affected by their sudden good fortune; the sharp and watchful gaze which they bent upon her frightened her, and that completed the business. She blushed, she became nervous and confused, and to the old people these were plain signs of guilt — guilt of some fearful sort or other — without doubt she was a spy and traitor. When they were alone again they began to piece many unrelated things together and get horrible results out of the combination. When things had got about to the worst, Richards was delivered of a sudden gasp, and his wife asked:

"Oh, what is it? — what is it?"

"The note — Burgess' note! Its language was sarcastic, I see it now." He quoted: "'At bottom you cannot respect me *knowing*, as you do, of *that matter* of which I am accused' — oh, it is perfectly plain, now, God help me! He knows that I know! You see the ingenuity of the phrasing. It was a trap — and like a fool, I walked into it. And Mary—?"

"Oh, it is dreadful — I know what you are going to say— he didn't return your transcript of the pretended test-remark."

"No — kept it to destroy us with. Mary, he has exposed us to some already. I know it — I know it well. I saw it in a dozen faces after church. Ah, he wouldn't answer our nod of recognition — *he* knew what he had been doing!"

In the night the doctor was called. The news went around in the morning that the old couple were rather seriously ill — prostrated by the exhausting excitement growing out of their great windfall, the congratulations, and the late hours, the doctor said. The town was sincerely distressed; for these old people were about all it had left to be proud of, now.

Two days later the news was worse. The old couple were delirious, and were doing strange things. By witness of the nurses, Richards had exhibited checks — for $8,500? No— for an amazing sum — $38,500! What could be the explanation of this gigantic piece of luck?

The following day the nurses had more news — and wonderful. They had concluded to hide the checks, lest harm come to them; but when they searched they were gone from under the patient's pillow — vanished away. The patient said:

"Let the pillow alone; what do you want?"

"We thought it best that the checks —"

"You will never see them again — they are destroyed.

They came from Satan. I saw the hell-brand on them, and I knew they were sent to betray me to sin." Then he fell to gabbling strange and dreadful things which were not clearly understandable, and which the doctor admonished them to keep to themselves.

Richards was right; the checks were never seen again.

A nurse must have talked in her sleep, for within two days the forbidden gabblings were the property of the town; and they were of a surprising sort. They seemed to indicate that Richards had been a claimant for the sack himself, and that Burgess had concealed that fact and then maliciously betrayed it.

Burgess was taxed with this and stoutly denied it. And he said it was not fair to attach weight to the chatter of a sick old man who was out of his mind. Still, suspicion was in the air, and there was much talk.

After a day or two it was reported that Mrs. Richards'

delirious deliveries were getting to be duplicates of her husband's. Suspicion flamed up into conviction, now, and the town's pride in the purity of its one undiscredited important citizen began to dim down and flicker toward extinction.

Six days passed, then came more news. The old couple were dying. Richards' mind cleared in his latest hour, and he sent for Burgess. Burgess said:

"Let the room be cleared. I think he wishes to say something in privacy."

"No!" said Richards; "I want witnesses. I want you all to hear my confession, so that I may die a man, and not a dog. I was clean — artificially — like the rest; and like the rest I fell when temptation came. I signed a lie, and claimed the miserable sack. Mr. Burgess remembered that I had done him a service, and in gratitude (and ignorance) he suppressed my claim and saved me. You know the thing that was charged against Burgess years ago. My testimony, and mine alone, could have cleared him, and I was a coward, and left him to suffer disgrace —"

"No — no — Mr. Richards, you —"

"My servant betrayed my secret to him —"

"No one has betrayed anything to me —"

— "and then he did a natural and justifiable thing, he repented of the saving kindness which he had done me, and he *exposed* me — as I deserved —"

"Never! — I make oath —"

"Out of my heart I forgive him."

Burgess' impassioned protestations fell upon deaf ears; the dying man passed away without knowing that once more he had done poor Burgess a wrong. The old wife died that night.

That last of the sacred Nineteen had fallen a prey to the fiendish sack; the town was stripped of the last rag of its ancient glory. Its mourning was not showy, but it was deep.

By act of the Legislature — upon prayer and petition—Hadleyburg was allowed to change its name to (never mind what — I will not give it away), and leave one word out of the motto that for many generations had graced the town's official seal.

It is an honest town once more, and the man will have to rise early that catches it napping again.

Mark Twain (1835-1910)

Mark Twain was the pen name of Samuel Longhorne Clemens, generally regarded as the greatest humorist in American literature. While appreciating the laughter and the enjoyment of life, his outlook was often pessimistic, and consequently his writings frequently portrayed this attitude.

Twain was born on November 30, 1835 in Florida, Missouri. At age four he moved with his family to Hannibal, Missouri, which he later immortalized in his classic book, *Tom Sawyer*, under the name of St. Petersburg. By age twelve, after experiencing the death of his father, Twain had grown tired of school. His adventurous spirit enticed him to travel extensively, taking him from St. Louis to New Orleans and eventually out West.

These extensive travels would ultimately provide Twain with some of his greatest stories, as he recalled everything from his days as a riverpilot on the Mississippi to his mining years and the lure of gold in California. Initially, however, it led him to a job as a dispatcher for the Virginia City "Territorial Express" in 1862. It is here where Clemens first signed himself as

Mark Twain, a riverboat term meaning two fathoms.

Thus began a spectacular literary career which would eventually produce such notable tales as: *Tom Sawyer*, *The Adventures of Huckleberry Finn*, *The Prince and the Pauper*, and *The Celebrated Jumping Frog of Calaveras County*. A career that for Twain made work indistinguishable from pleasure, for as he commented that while others toiled, "I spent a lifetime of delightful idleness."

Mark Twain, despite his extraordinary sense of humor spent the last twenty years of his life embittered by misfortune and plagued with bad health. As a result his writing style began to take on the attitude that lived within him. His works began to search for a moral and social reform for society, hoping to overcome what he believed was the selfish nature of man.

Samuel Clemens died on April 21, 1910 at the age of 74, leaving behind works that will as he once dreamed, forever, "excite the laughter of God's creatures."